GOODNIGHT, GOODNIGHT

Eve Rice
GOODNIGHT, GOODNIGHT

Puffin Books

For the Mattisons—
Sr., Jr., and Jr. Jr.

Goodnight came over
the rooftops slowly.

"Goodnight," said the man
in the window in the tower,

"Goodnight," said the
chestnut vendor down below,

and a lady coming home,

and a mama to her baby,

while one little cat on the
roof all alone said,

But all over town, Goodnight was

creeping slowly with the dark.

"Goodnight," said a man to
his parrot on a perch,

and a lady on TV
to anyone at all,

and the fireman nodded
when the big policeman called,

"Goodnight, Harry."
"Goodnight."

"Goodnight," said the woman
sitting sipping tea

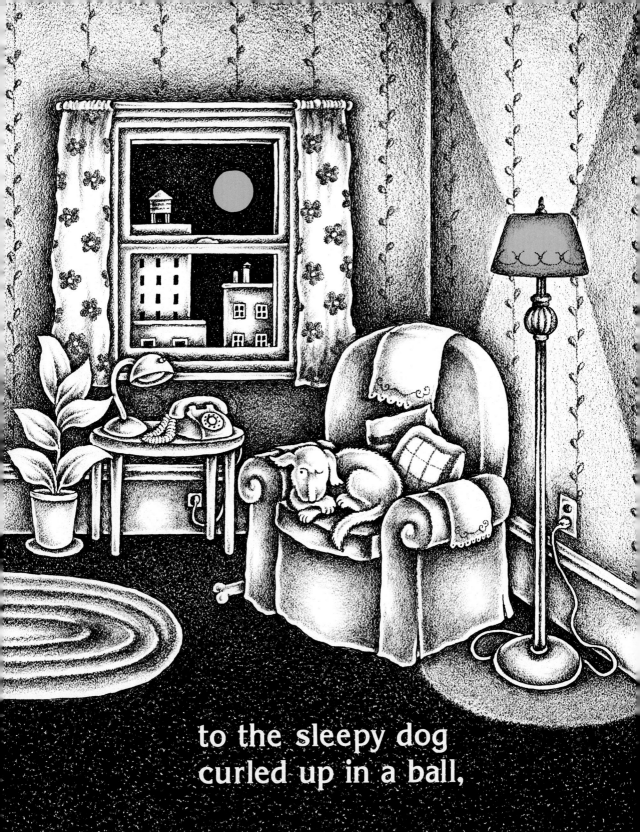

to the sleepy dog
curled up in a ball,

while up on the roof,
the little cat meowed so softly,

But Goodnight came here

and Goodnight went there,
all over town.

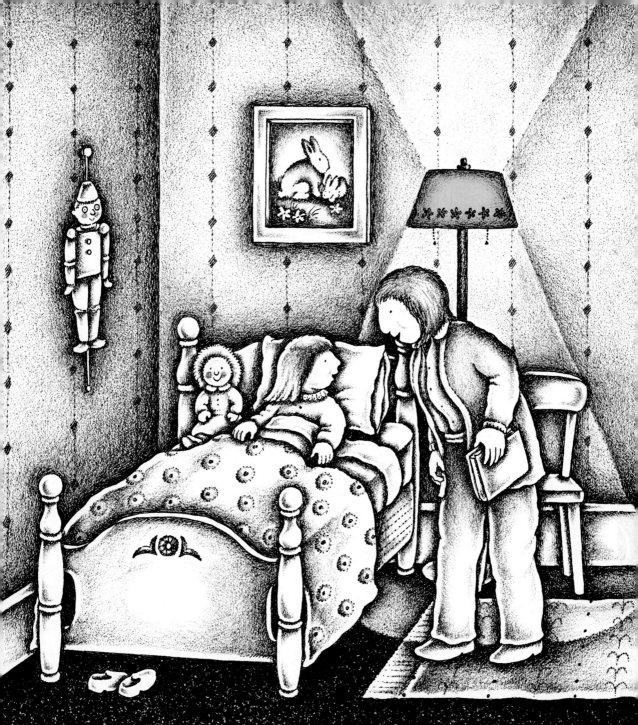

"Goodnight," said the girl
when her mother finished reading.

"Goodnight," said her mother
and her father and her brother.

Goodnight settled softly

on the buildings all around,

while up on the roof,
one little cat purred

to his mother who had found him,
"Goodnight, Mother Cat."

"Goodnight."